R

THE BEST
WORST DAY EVER

Sophy Henn

SIMON & SCHUSTER

London   New York   Sydney   Toronto   New Delhi

for Ben
Here's to the best
days ever, ever!

SIMON & SCHUSTER
First published in Great Britain in 2021 by Simon & Schuster UK Ltd
1st Floor, 222 Gray's Inn Road, London WC1X 8HB

Text and illustrations copyright © 2021 Sophy Henn

The right of Sophy Henn to be identified as the author
and illustrator of this work has been asserted by her in accordance
with the Copyright, Designs and Patents Act, 1988

A CIP catalogue record for this book is available from
the British Library upon request

ISBN: 978-1-4711-9423-8 (HB)
ISBN: 978-1-4711-9422-1 (PB)
ISBN: 978-1-4711-9424-5 (eBook)

Printed in China
1 3 5 7 9 10 8 6 4 2

Arthur's day was not going at all
as he had imagined it would.

It was quite simply the worst day ever.

"**No!**" stomped Arthur.

"**NO!!**" huffed Arthur.

And then he **roared.**

Arthur became absolutely
certain that he couldn't do
a single thing right,

so he **stomped**

and he **huffed**

and he **roared** some more.

But that didn't help at all.

There's nothing for it, thought Arthur.
I will just have to run away.

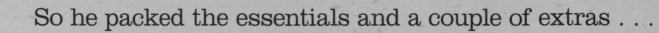

So he packed the essentials and a couple of extras . . .

and Arthur ran away.

He ran and he ran, as far as he could,
past the shed and very nearly to the end
of the garden.

Then he stopped.

Arthur flopped down on the ground and thought about how it was all so **very** dreadful.

Then Arthur wondered how long he had been gone because he was feeling rather hungry and almost certain his hair had grown.

Maybe I should go back home, he thought.

Everyone is probably missing me by now and feeling terribly sad.

But when Arthur turned to go, he saw that he really must have been gone for a very long while as a big, dark forest had grown up between him and home.

Well, there's no time to go around it, thought Arthur.
So I had better be brave and go through it instead.

Arthur felt nervous and not at all sure.
The forest was **SO** big and **SO** dark and
made strange noises all around him.

They got louder

and louder

and louder . . .

until all of a sudden . . .

. . . there was a Bear.

And this Bear was stomping

all over the place.

So Arthur stomped all over the place too
and they both **stamped** and **stomped**
until there was nowhere left to **stomp** at all.

But then . . .

. . . a **stomp** turned into
a **skip**,

which turned into
a **wiggle**

and before they knew it,
Arthur and the Bear
were **dancing**.

"I think I like skipping and wiggling better than stamping and stomping," said Arthur, and the Bear couldn't help but agree.

So Arthur and the Bear skipped and wiggled on through the forest.

Then quite by surprise . . .

. . . there was an Elephant.

And this particular Elephant was having
a huff and all in all looked quite put out.

So Arthur huffed too and they both huffed and they puffed until they almost went pop.

But then . . .

. . . a huff and a puff turned into

a toot and a hoot

and before they could stop, Arthur and
the Elephant were playing a wonderful tune.

"Tooting and hooting is much nicer

than huffing and even puffing," said Arthur,

and Elephant nodded, because, well, of course it was.

On they danced and tooted and hooted for what seemed like forever. Then, quite out of the blue, there was a Lion.

The Lion roared . . .

Arthur **roared** back.

Then Arthur and the Lion
roared and **roared** and
roared themselves silly.

But then a roar turned into a **yodel** and
the **yodel** turned into a song

and all of a sudden, Arthur and the Lion
found themselves singing along.

Arthur told the Lion he much preferred singing to
roaring but the Lion had to have a bit of a think about that.

Then Arthur and the Bear
and the Lion and the
Elephant danced and
sang and tooted
and hooted on
through the forest.

And very soon they forgot about the forest
being big and dark as they were far too busy
having a wonderful, happy time.

In fact, they were so busy they
very nearly missed the back door.

"Oh, I suppose I am home," said Arthur.
"But maybe I am having too much fun
with all of you to go home now."

And while everyone agreed that it had been the **best** worst day ever, the Bear had a bubble bath waiting, the Elephant was very tired and the Lion had to go home for his tea.

"But . . . what if everyone is **extra** cross with me now for running away?" said Arthur.

But of course they weren't.

In fact, it was almost as if he'd never been gone . . .

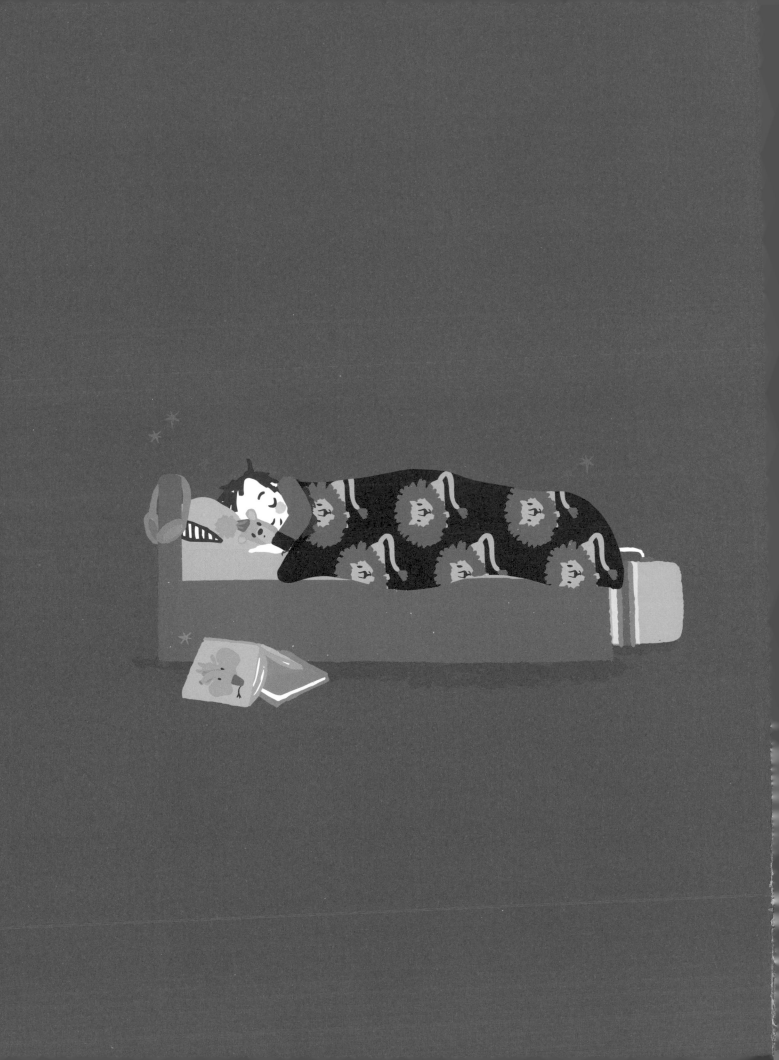